HEA Title II-A

D1030031

SAD-FACED BOY

SLUMBER WAS POUNDING THE BIG OLD DRUM

F
B

Sad-Faced Boy

By ARNA BONTEMPS

Illustrated by VIRGINIA LEE BURTON

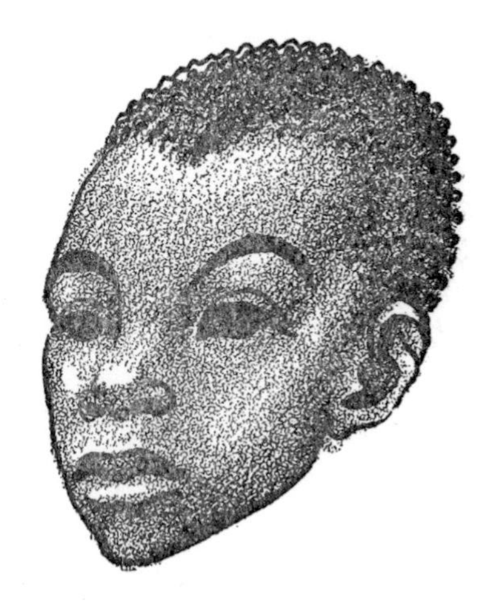

BOSTON
HOUGHTON MIFFLIN COMPANY
The Riverside Press Cambridge

IMMACULATA COLLEGE
HAMBURG, NEW YORK

24, 126

COPYRIGHT, 1937, BY ARNA BONTEMPS

ALL RIGHTS RESERVED INCLUDING THE RIGHT TO REPRODUCE
THIS BOOK OR PARTS THEREOF IN ANY FORM

TWELFTH PRINTING R

The Riverside Press
CAMBRIDGE · MASSACHUSETTS
PRINTED IN THE U.S.A.

Table of Contents

I. Mr. Railroad Train 1
II. Harlem 9
III. Uncle Jasper Tappin 17
IV. Sugar Hill 26
V. Eighth Avenue 37
VI. Harlem Boys 49
VII. The Library 61
VIII. "Now Guess Where I'm Going" 71
IX. The Parade 80
X. The Dozier Brothers 88
XI. Bright Lights 95
XII. Abie 104
XIII. Ripe Persimmons 112

Illustrations

Slumber was pounding the big old drum for all it was worth *Frontispiece*

Slumber saw a tuft of gray wool on top of an old wrinkled head 20

"Where you learn that music, you sad-faced boy, you?" 32

He was going to make those white tiles shine or else scrub a hole in them 38

The boys turned a corner and began to feel a little safer 48

"Now how you going to get back home?" 58

"This is the time. Let's strike it up, big shorty" 102

"I'm going on back down home to Alabama" 116

I

Mr. Railroad Train

SLUMBER, the sad-faced boy, drew his harmonica lightly across his lips. What should he play next? Ho-hum, it was almost too hot to think.

He was lying on the platform of the freight station, his cap pulled down to shade his eyes from the sun, one leg hanging over the edge. He had played all the songs he knew two or three times each and he was ready to play them again, but this heat was simply too much.

It was not that Slumber was not used to hot weather. He knew what it was to work in the fields when old Mr. Sun was putting out all the strength he had. He was used to hoeing cotton when the ground was hot enough to fry an egg. Once he had driven a mule to a cultivator when the sun beat down so powerfully it gave the old critter blind staggers. But lying on the freight station platform like this was something else again. It was all Slumber could do to keep from going to sleep.

Rags and Willie were already asleep, one on a bale of cotton, the other stretched across some sacks of grain. Slumber knew that they were depending on him to wake them if anything happened, and that was why he couldn't stop playing his harmonica. Ho-hum, what should he play next? Maybe he would try "Back, Back, Train, and Get Your Heavy Load." That was as good a song as any, and at the same time it gave him a chance to think about something that was on his mind right now.

Slumber commenced patting his foot to get the time. When he felt that he had it right, he put the little instrument to his mouth and let the tune trickle out.

He was a sad-faced boy, that Slumber. He was sad-faced and he never laughed. He always thought about sad things like sick kittens and cows who had seen their pretty calves sold to the butcher and buzzards sitting on fence posts because they were too tired to fly any more. His older brother Rags and his younger brother

Willie were not the same; but when these two laughed, Slumber could almost never see anything funny. He was a sad boy.

Sometimes, of course, on days like today, when he had powerful thoughts in his head, he felt a bit happier inside. Neither Slumber nor Rags nor Willie had told a soul, but great things were about to happen. The three brothers were not just hanging around the freight station for nothing. No, sir. They had business there.

Just before he went to sleep on that bale of cotton, Rags had whispered to Slumber: "Keep on blowing that thing, son. I'm going to take me a little nap now. If anybody come walking along here and looking at us kind of funny, you just swing your foot and blow that harmonica like nothing ain't never happened and nothing ain't never going to happen. Understand?"

"I hear what you say, and I know what you mean. Take your nap, big shorty," Slumber whispered.

Little Willie, opening his eyes suddenly, added, "But if you hears that big choo-choo, make me know it, bubber — give me the high sign right quick."

"Shut your eyes, little half-pint. I'll give you the high sign when the time come."

Slumber patted his foot and played his song. The other boys had been asleep a long time now. A good many people had passed the platform — a freight agent, a farmer, a policeman, and several others that Slumber had not raised his head to see. Nobody stopped to ask what the boys were doing on the freight platform. Why, anyone could *see* that Slumber was swinging his foot and playing his harmonica; anybody who wasn't blind could tell that Rags and Willie were sound asleep.

Another hour passed. Then suddenly the old lazy freight train peeped its mouse's nose around the bend and began puffing down the stretch.

"Well, sir, here we be," Slumber whispered. "It's time to part your hair in the middle of your head and put on your long-tailed blue."

Rags raised his head, blinking in the sun. "What's that you talk about, son?"

"Leaving time, big shorty. Keep one eye shut and one eye open now. Yonder comes our train. Five-ten minutes from now I aim to be New York bound. What about you?"

"I'm with you this time, son."

"Me, too," Willie whispered, excited. He slipped one hand over his eyes and peeped through the fingers.

The old freighter pulled into the station and stopped. Then it began backing and switching to pick up some cars that had been standing on a side rail. Later it stopped at the platform again while the trainmen gave the engine water and the station men loaded the stacked boxes and sacks into cars.

Slumber continued to play his harmonica, but he wasn't paying much attention to the music now. He was trying to make up his mind where he would ride. There seemed to be about twenty-five or thirty cars to choose from, but of course some of them were loaded too full and some were closed. Slumber set his eyes on one that had a door swinging open. It appeared to be empty, except for scraps of paper and packing straw scattered over the floor.

The men finished loading the freight, and the engine blew its whistle up front.

Slumber slipped his harmonica into an overall pocket.

"Come on, you all," he said, getting up.

The boys started down the platform. Slumber noticed that nearly every box car had people in it. Somebody had told him that the railroad company occasionally allowed folks to ride their freight trains when times were hard and poor people didn't have enough money to pay for tickets on the passenger trains. That was the way Slumber had heard it, and now he began to think that maybe it was true.

"Where we going to get on at?" Willie asked.

"I see one that looks good to me way down yonder," Slumber said. "The door's hanging open, and I don't believe anybody's in it."

"I see the one you mean," Rags said. "Down there near the tail."

"Yes, let's hurry."

The train was beginning to move slowly. The boys set out on a run. When they reached the door of their car, they had to turn around and start running the way the train was going. The door was a little high for Willie, so Slumber and Rags had to help him up. Slumber hopped next. By that time Rags was running so fast his feet scarcely touched the ground. When Slumber was out of the way, however, he made a leap and landed inside the car.

The boys closed the big sliding door part-way and began looking around. There was nothing inside but heaps of packing straw and scraps of torn paper. The lazy old train was picking up speed rapidly now, and the closed box car had a roaring sound inside.

"You sure this the New York train, bubber?" Willie asked, peeping out the door crack and watching the red Alabama country slip by.

"This the right track," Rags said. "We might have to change trains somewheres up the line, but we on the right road."

"I always did want to see New York," Slumber said, looking even sadder than usual. "They tell me there's some powerful tall buildings up there."

He took his harmonica from his pocket and began playing again. Willie rolled on a pile of paper and straw. Rags leaned against a wall, looking out the door crack.

"You're bearing down on that old mouth organ, son. How come you play so sweet now?"

Slumber paused. "I'm on my way, big shorty, and it make me feel kind of good inside."

Rags patted his foot to the tune.

"Blow your whistle, Mr. Railroad Train," he murmured. "Me and my two bubbers is all got the itching feet. We got them bad, and we aims to see that place they call Harlem. Blow your whistle, sir. Take us away from here, if you please."

Of course, the engine could not hear Rags, but something seemed to get into his old steel hide about that time. Maybe he was stung by a bee. Maybe a country boy frightened him by waving a red rag. Slumber had no idea how it came about, but just then the old creature started blowing his whistle for all he was worth. He kicked up his heels and started running fit to break his neck.

"Seem like this old train is in a hurry," Willie said.

"It can't go too fast for me," Slumber said, taking the harmonica out of his mouth for a moment.

"Me neither," Rags said.

II

Harlem

THERE was no doubt that the train on which they left Alabama was fast, but Slumber and Rags and Willie soon learned that it was not going to New York. Neither was the one to which they changed at Knoxville. And the last leg of the journey, from Philadelphia to New York, was not made by train at all, but by a truck. For it was in Philadelphia that a police officer pulled the boys out of another box car they had just boarded and explained that they would have to find another way to travel from there on. It was his business to see that no boys named Slumber or Rags or Willie were on the freight trains that left the yard where he was stationed.

With the truck-driver it was different. He had brought a load of furniture down from New York and was just getting ready to start back with his empty truck.

"Sure," he said, "hop on if you're going my way. But don't be poking your head out. I'm not supposed to carry riders. Lay down on them quilts and things in there. It's just a pile of stuff we use for padding between the furniture to keep the good pieces from getting scratched."

That made Slumber feel a little better. He had begun to be sad again, thinking he might not get to New York after all, but the truck-driver's words made a lot of difference. The boys climbed into the big van and buried themselves in the heaps of soft padding. Slumber's face was still long and sorrowful, but inside he was feeling better — much better.

And that was the strange thing about Slumber. Even when he felt a little happier, his face remained sad. In fact, the happier Slumber felt the sadder he looked. That was why so many old folks looked at him and said, "Boy, you is a caution for sure." They didn't often see a youngster just like Slumber.

The boys had been on the way two days, and the country had begun to look much different, but it was hard to realize that they were a thousand miles from home. Yet it was true. They had traveled a thousand miles and were aiming to go farther. It was late at night when the truck left Philadelphia.

The home the boys had left in Alabama was just a small brown cabin, not much taller than the high green corn that grew around it. Closing his eyes as he lay on the floor of the truck, Slumber could see it very plain, and he remembered that there were some pretty things about his home, things that he might tell the city folks when he reached New York. There was, first of all, a row of sunflowers his mama had planted on one side. At the back doorstep there was the lilac bush. Slumber could tell his Uncle Jasper Tappin, who lived in the part of New York City called Harlem, how sweet the world smelled when that lilac bush bloomed. He could tell him how the family stuck eggshells on its bare twigs in winter, making the bush look like an egg tree. Then there was the vine that covered the front part of the cabin. Slumber thought it would be hard to describe the blue trumpet-shaped flowers that hung in clusters like bunches of grapes on that vine. Yes, indeed, it would surely be hard to describe, he thought, but Uncle Jasper Tappin would have to be told about it just the same. Slumber would have to find the words.

Uncle Jasper Tappin would have to be told about the view from the doorsteps, also. He would have to be told how the fields of cotton seemed to roll like waves; how on every little rise, about half a mile apart, there was a clump of trees and under the green clump a low brown cabin squatting down in the shade like a hen with chicks. Oh, there were so many things to tell an uncle in a big city. Slumber remembered the wild peaches and the plums and the cherries, the swamp and the bullfrogs and the snakes, the buzzards and the owls and the hawks — so many things, so many things to tell Uncle Jasper Tappin in New York.

The truck sped on. Soon all the boys were asleep.

Slumber slept hard, but he woke suddenly, hearing a great clamor and jangle and confusion outside. The truck was moving slowly, starting and stopping, starting and stopping. Inside, the big moving van was streaked with daylight that came through a tiny front window and through cracks in the rear doors. The clamor on the outside grew louder and louder. There were bells ringing, motors popping, wheels rattling, voices shouting, and overhead a roar like thunder. Slumber's eyes grew larger; his face became so long and sad he seemed about ready to cry. Where in the world had the truck-driving man carried them?

The other boys were sitting up by now. Each looked troubled and afraid. Then suddenly the truck stopped, and the driver called through the small open window.

"Say, big fellows, you still back there?"

"Yes," Rags answered. "We still here."

"Well, here is your Harlem."

"Oh," Slumber said softly. "So that's what I been hearing."

"Folks up here sure is noisy a plenty," Willie said.

"This is where you wanted to come," the truck-driving man answered. "And here you are. You got to get out now."

He went around to the rear of the truck, swung one of the doors aloose, and the three boys climbed to the ground. Slumber rolled his eyes sadly, looked all around him and up in the air.

"So this is it?" he whispered. "New York, hunh?"

"Harlem," the driver said. "That's just one part of New York."

Tall buildings rose on every side. There were car tracks in the street and car tracks on a trestle above the street. On those upper tracks elevated trains passed with a roar like thunder. So many wagons and trucks and automobiles and street-cars jostled down below that Slumber expected them to smash into one another any minute.

"I never seen so many cars and the like," Slumber said in his unhappy voice.

"You haven't seen half of it yet," the driver said, getting back into the seat of his truck. "There are car tracks down under the ground in this man's city. Ask somebody to show them to you sometime."

"Yes, sir, I sure will," Slumber said.

The truck drove away.

Slumber and Rags and Willie stood on the street corner for a long while without speaking a word. Their mouths dropped open and their eyes got bigger and bigger. They looked at everything on the ground, turning slowly round and round as if they were just waking from sleep. Then they raised their faces and looked up at the tall buildings and the elevated trestle over-head. Still they said nothing. Harlem was just too wonderful for words.

A few minutes later they commenced walking. And as they walked they passed first a grocery store with fresh fruits and green vegetables displayed in the front. The boys paused to get a good look. What were those things like big red bananas? What did folks want with so many kinds of cabbage? Where did they get those funny-looking pears with skins like a watermelon?

"Harlem is wonderful," Rags said.

They were walking again, and Slumber was shaking his head slowly.

"True," he murmured as they came to a fish market. "True, what you say, big shorty. True."

The three lined up against the glass window of the fish market. In tubs and bins and barrels and troughs and buckets and on trays the fish were spread out so that they could be seen. There were some kinds that Slumber recognized, like catfish and crayfish and oysters and perch and eels; and lying on the floor there were some big old terrapins that he knew, too. But there were even more kinds that he did not know.

"We better keep walking," Rags said after they had seen everything in the fish market.

"Where we walking to?" Willie asked, taking his older brother's hand.

"I got the number in my pocket here," Rags told him. "Uncle Jasper Tappin will be mighty surprised when he see us."

They walked a little faster now, passing furniture stores and pawnshops and beauty parlors and barber shops and drug stores and lunch counters until they reached a corner and turned into a side street where there were no more store fronts.

"Now we can start looking for Uncle Jasper Tappin's number," Slumber said softly.

"Yes," Rags whispered. "That's what we can do now."

III

Uncle Jasper Tappin

SOON the street on which the boys were walking ran up a hill that overlooked a park. A row of tall apartment houses stood on the left side of the street, and on the other side, beyond the walk, there was an iron fence that kept children from falling down the hill into the park — which, the way this hill was made, would have been a long hard fall with plenty of rocks to bump on. Slumber and his brothers could not see the numbers on the houses from the fence side of the street, so they crossed over and began looking from the building side for the apartment house in which Uncle Jasper Tappin lived.

"Are you looking at those numbers good, big bubber?" Willie asked, after they had walked another block.

"I'm looking good," Rags answered. "I'm looking at everything we pass, but the number is 400, and we just in the three's now."

The number they were seeking turned out to be the last building on the hill and the tallest of them all.

"This must not be the place," Slumber murmured sadly. "Uncle Jasper Tappin wouldn't hardly be living in a building big as this one. This building must be near about a mile high."

"It's high a plenty, but it ain't no mile. Besides, Uncle Jasper Tappin said he lives in the basement," Rags said. "Just keep on following me. I'll get you there, son."

Slumber and Willie believed their big brother knew what he was talking about, so they walked behind him as he went down a few steps and around some turns till he came to a door with the word JANITOR written on it.

"You knock, Slumber," Rags said.

"No, let Willie," Slumber said.

"I'm afraid," Willie said. "You knock, Rags."

"Never mind, I will," Slumber said, putting his knuckles against the door.

Uncle Jasper Tappin did not come at once, and the boys began to feel discouraged. Still Slumber continued to rap on the door. His face became longer and sadder than usual, but he did not stop knocking.

"Uncle Jasper Tappin must be moved somewheres else," Willie said, almost ready to cry.

"No, I think he still lives here," Rags told him. "Keep on knocking, Slumber."

Slumber did not stop. And finally, when his knuckles were just beginning to feel sore from the knocking, Slumber heard footsteps inside, heavy footsteps coming slowly to the door. All three of the boys stood back and waited. Then, a moment later, the door cracked open just a tiny bit. Slowly, inch by inch, the crack got wider. Finally Slumber saw a tuft of gray wool on top of an old wrinkled head. After that he saw two old eyes blinking in the crack of the door.

"Well, you scamps!" an old cracked voice said. "Was you trying to break my door down, knocking like all that?"

"No, sir," Slumber answered. "We wasn't aiming to break the door."

The door opened a little wider, and the boys could see the old man a trifle better.

"Whose boys is you all? I ain't never seen you before, has I?"

"We is Rags and Slumber and Willie Dozier, Uncle Jasper Tappin. Don't you know us?" the boys said.

"No you ain't.'

"Yes we is," Slumber said.

"Aw, you's trying to fool me — you old sad-faced boy, you."

"Uncle Jasper Tappin, here is the letter what you writ to us," Rags said, taking the wrinkled envelope from his pocket.

Uncle Jasper Tappin's eyes got round.

"My letter, hunh? Well, dog my cats, I reckon you is the boys then. My-oh-me, but look how big — mighty near big as menfolks. Come on inside here and talk to me. Do your mama know you is way up here in Harlem?"

The boys followed him into the apartment, but none of them wanted to answer his last question.

"This ain't like the house we live in," Rags said, trying to change the subject.

"Never mind about that," Uncle Jasper Tappin answered. "I say do your mama know you is way up here in Harlem?"

"We aim to write her a letter right soon."

SLUMBER SAW A TUFT OF GRAY WOOL ON TOP OF AN OLD WRINKLED HEAD

Slumber said in his sad voice. "We aim to do that for a fact, Uncle Jasper Tappin. We aim to do it right soon. We didn't have time to tell her just exactly where we was going."

Uncle Jasper Tappin followed the boys into his little sitting room. There he stood over them for a long time shaking his head and saying nothing.

"You done run away from home," he told them finally. "You scamps has just naturally picked up and left your good old mama and pappy down yonder in Alabama."

This made Slumber feel so sad tears began running down his face.

"That's what we done done, Uncle Jasper Tappin. What you going to do to us?" he said.

Again Uncle Jasper Tappin had to shake his head and think for a long time.

"Don't send us back, sir," little Willie said. "We want to see New York. Please don't send us back."

Then suddenly old Uncle Jasper Tappin thought of something that made him laugh. He covered his face with his hands so the boys couldn't see how hard he was laughing, but they could hear his chuckles plain.

"What you laughing at, Uncle Jasper Tappin?" Slumber asked, his long face still wet with tears.

"N-nothing, son—just thinking about something funny."

"Funny like what?" Rags asked.

"Well, I'll tell you. I was thinking about another little scamp, just such another rascal as you all, who picked up and ran away from that same cabin about fifty year ago."

"What was his name?" Slumber asked.

"His name? Why, his name was Jasper Tappin Dozier. Hee-hee-hee!"

That made all the boys laugh, too. So Uncle Jasper Tappin, their father's oldest brother, had run away without asking his mama, too. Now that *was* something to laugh about. It made them all feel as if they knew their uncle much better, too.

"Well, what you going to do with us now?" Slumber said, still a trifle worried.

"I'm going to take you up here in this big old apartment house and put you to work. That's what I'm going to do. I'm the superintendent of this building."

"And you won't make us go back home?" Willie said.

"Well, maybe not just yet. Not before you see New York, I reckon. Besides, I need to go back to Alabama myself, you know. I haven't ever been back to tell my old mama I's sorry for running away. I'm got to do that pretty soon, and I reckon I'd just as well keep you all here till I get ready to go."

"I'm ready to start cleaning up this old apartment house right now, me," Rags said.

"No, not just yet," Uncle Jasper Tappin told him. "You got to have something to eat first. After that you got to sit down and write your mama a letter so she'll know where you is. I'll have your Aunt Ludy write a note and put in with it."

"Where'bouts is Aunt Ludy?" Slumber asked.

"She just out buying us some dinner, but I 'spect she'll have to go back again when she see who all we going to have for dinner. He-he-he!"

"He-he-he!" Slumber said, smiling for the first

time since he left the state of Alabama. "He-he-he!"

The other boys laughed, too. It had been nearly a week since they had a warm dinner.

A few moments later a large woman opened the door and came in without knocking. It was Aunt Ludy. She left her packages in the kitchen and continued up the hall to the front room where the boys were still laughing with Uncle Jasper Tappin.

"Well, sir, who are all these strange gentlemen?" she asked smiling.

Uncle Jasper Tappin explained everything to her in a few words. Then he suggested that perhaps she would have to go back and get more greens and back bones for dinner, since there would be so many more mouths to feed. She agreed, but before leaving she thought of something she wanted to say to the three boys.

"When was the last time you all had a nice warm bath?" she asked.

Slumber looked at Rags and Rags looked at Willie. They couldn't say exactly when it had been — certainly not since they left Alabama.

"Well, now," said Aunt Ludy, "that's what

FB
24,126

I thought. Jasper Tappin, you can get them some bath towels and show them how to turn on the hot and cold water. By the time I get back, I want every one of you to be ready to sit at the table."

"We haven't got any clean clothes to put on," Rags suggested.

"You do what I say. We'll have to see what we can do about the clothes."

IMMACULATA COLLEGE
HAMBURG, NEW YORK

IV

Sugar Hill

SLUMBER stretched out in the warm water of his bath. Rags and Willie had already dried themselves and put on the clean clothes that Uncle Jasper Tappin went out and got for them. Slumber's new things were hanging on a nail, waiting for him. As soon as he could get himself clean, dinner would be ready. Aunt Ludy had already called from the kitchen to remind him of that. And there she was calling again.

"Hurry up, you old slow poke boy. Remember you're in Harlem now. You got to get a move on."

Slumber heard what she said, but he couldn't get a move on. The warm bath felt too good. He had never been in a tub like this one, and he had begun to think that a bath tub was just about the finest thing in the world. He stood up and soaped himself all over again. Then once more he rolled in the water, washing the soap from his body. Yes, a bath tub was a fine thing for sure. Ho-hum, and the warm water was fine, too. It made you feel like closing your eyes and staying there a long, long time. Yes, ho-hum. Slumber closed his eyes. It would just be for a minute. He felt so comfortable in the long tub, the warm water. In one more minute he'd open his eyes and get out of the tub. Ho-hum!

But a minute passed and Slumber had not moved. Two minutes passed, five minutes, fifteen, *twenty-five* minutes! Uncle Jasper Tappin and Rags and Willie took their places at the table. Aunt Ludy started bringing things from the kitchen to the dining room. As she went back and forth, she called to Slumber three times. "Come on, slow poke, we just about ready to eat. Come on, you sad-faced boy, I'm putting the dishes on the table. Hurry up, you Slumber, you."

"Wonder what's keeping that boy," Uncle Jasper Tappin said.

"Maybe he got drowned in that bath tub,"

Willie said. "Slumber can't swim so good, you know."

The others laughed at little Willie, but they were tired of waiting for Slumber. After a few more minutes Aunt Ludy lost her patience.

"Jasper Tappin," she said, "go in there and see what's holding that boy back. The dinner's going to be all cold."

So Uncle Jasper Tappin went to the bathroom door and opened it. Slumber was not drowned. Nothing was holding him back, either. He was just fast asleep in the bath tub.

"Well, dog my cats," Uncle Jasper Tappin exclaimed. "This beats Jack Robinson, and *he* beat the *band*. Gone to sleep in the bath tub, and all of us sitting at the table waiting for him. You Slumber! You better get up from there, boy. Don't you know the dinner will get cold? Wake up, I say. Rags and Willie and me is about starving. We can't wait for you to take a nap in the bath tub."

Slumber opened his eyes, rolled them sadly. Ho-hum, the warm water felt *so* good.

"I didn't go to do it, Uncle Jasper Tappin. For a fact, I really didn't. But this old bath tub feels so good, this old water is so warm and nice, this old soap smells so good, I just couldn't help it. But I'm coming directly now. I'll be there before you can bat your eye. You just see if I don't."

It did not take Slumber long to get himself dried and dressed, but by the time he reached the table the others were eating.

"Well, that's a new something you bringing up here," Aunt Ludy said, "going to sleep in the bath tub. But never mind, you'll learn to keep your eyes open if you stay up here long."

The dinner was good. The boys finished eating and Uncle Jasper Tappin pushed his chair back from the table.

"Well, has everybody got a plenty?" he asked.

"Yes, sir," the boys murmured.

"No more greens and back bone? No more salad? No more rice and gravy? No more strawberry short cake?"

"No more nothing," Slumber said slowly. "We can't hardly move now. This the best dinner we had in a month or more."

"Well, I'm glad you got enough," Aunt Ludy

said. "We'll just have something light for supper when you come in this evening."

"It's most too late to do any real work today," Uncle Jasper Tappin said. "Yet and still we can look the apartment house over and get you ready to do some real helping later on."

The boys followed him out to the elevator and Uncle Jasper Tappin rang the bell.

"Isn't that an elevator over there, too?" Slumber asked as they waited for the door to open.

"Yes," Uncle Jasper Tappin said. "That's what you call the service elevator. We use that for hauling freight and trash. But we're not working just now, so we'll go up on the regular elevator if that boy ever gets here."

The door opened finally, and the three boys stepped in ahead of Uncle Jasper Tappin.

The elevator boy wore a red uniform with large gold buttons.

"Which floor?" he asked.

"Thirteen," Uncle Jasper Tappin told him.

The thirteenth floor was really the roof. The boys, walking behind their uncle, went outside and looked at the blue sky. Then they walked to the front wall and looked down on the park.

They looked at all the rooftops of Harlem and the streets far below. There was so much to see Slumber scarcely knew what to look at.

"This here is New York?" he whispered.

"Yes," Uncle Jasper Tappin said. "This is New York. See up there . . . That's the downtown part."

"What's that great tall building?" Rags asked.

"The Empire State Building, that is. And up this-a-way is the Bronx. And all down below, all around the park there and up that-a-way towards that other park yonder — well, that's all Harlem."

"There's a plenty to see," Slumber said.

"You mighty right about that. More than you can see in one day, or one week either," the old man said.

Slumber slipped his mouth organ from his pocket and began playing softly. The other two boys leaned their elbows on the wall and continued to look at the sights. After a while Slumber paused to rub his lips and think up a new song to play.

"I always wanted to see New York," he told Uncle Jasper Tappin.

"Well, you boys just look around for a while," the old man said. "I'm going down to see if the halls are all clean. I'll be back soon."

Slumber began a new tune when the three boys were alone.

"What that you playing now?" Willie asked. "I never heard you play that before."

"No, I reckon you never did," Slumber said. "I'm just making it up as I go. It's a song about three country boys in a great big city."

"About you and me and Rags?"

Slumber just nodded his head. He was playing again and he couldn't stop to talk. Soon he began patting his foot. The music trickled out sweetly. Willie sat down and began drumming on a tin can with two sticks. Rags put his fingers in his mouth and whistled like an old train whistling as it leaves Alabama. He shuffled his feet slowly, began dancing.

As he danced lazily to the music of Slumber and Willie, Rags began to think of words to go with the music.

"Aw, blow your whistle, Mister Railroad Train," he said. "Blow your whistle on the

'WHERE YOU LEARN THAT MUSIC, YOU SAD-FACED BOY, YOU?'

Dixie line. Sun in the sky, not a tree in sight. Country boys in a big man's town."

Slumber was playing for all he was worth by now. Willie was trying to beat holes in his tin can. Rags made the sound of that train whistle again and continued to shuffle drowsily. "Aw, blow your whistle on the Dixie line."

Then suddenly Slumber observed that someone else was listening to the music. It was nobody he knew, nobody he had ever seen before. She wore a little checkered skirt with suspender-like straps over the shoulders, and there was a red tam on her head. She had come out of the door quietly, but now that she was near the music, she began to clap her hands. The girl watched the boys for a while, then clicked her heels and made a few little steps of her own.

"Where you learn that music, you sad-faced boy, you?" she said pleasantly. "Who taught you how to blow that harp?"

Slumber shook his head.

"Don't ask me nothing," he told her, pausing. "Don't ask me a thing. We just got to Harlem and we can't sit down."

"Well, listen to me," the girl said, putting

her feet down emphatically. "You do right well yourself, old sad-faced boy, but your two brothers here need to learn something if they want to play music in this town. Let me show you how to beat that drum there, little bubber. Move over." She shoved Willie aside. Then, turning to Rags, she added, "When I get through here, I'll show you how to dance, tall boy."

Willie gave up his sticks reluctantly. Slumber rubbed his lips and knocked the harmonica against his knee. Then he began playing again.

"See there," the girl said, catching the rhythm and tapping the can like a real drummer. "It's easy when you know how."

"Hum!" Willie said unpleasantly. "Hum!"

Anybody could see that the happy-faced little girl could do more good drum beating in a minute than Willie could do in an hour. Even Willie could see that, so there was nothing for him to say but *hum*.

Rags had quit dancing and stood beside his small brother observing carefully every move the newcomer made as she beat the traps to Slumber's harmonica playing. When he was thoroughly convinced that she knew her business and that there was no fault to be found with her playing, he said softly, "What's your name, anyhow?"

"Daisy Bee," she said. A little later she asked, "Where did you boys come from?"

"Way down the line," Rags told her. "Alabama. We come up here to see our Uncle Jasper Tappin. We heard a lot of talk about New York and Harlem."

"Oh, he's your uncle! Well, did you ever hear about Sugar Hill?" she asked.

The boys shook their heads.

"Where'bouts is that?" Willie said.

"Right here," Daisy Bee explained. She stopped and pointed with one of the drum sticks. "All the hill up on this side of the park is Sugar Hill. This is about the best row of apartment houses in Harlem, and this one that we're on is the tallest of all. Look down that way and you can see."

Slumber paused to look with the others.

"Oh, yes."

"But we haven't got time for a lot of looking now," Daisy Bee said, getting up from the floor. "Take your drum back, little bubber. Let me see if you can beat it any better since I showed you how. Strike up another tune, sad-faced boy. Come on, tall boy, let me show you how to get those steps right. Maybe I can make something out of you three yet."

The boys didn't exactly like the way Daisy Bee talked. She was high-handed. She simply told you what she wanted you to do and you had to do it. She didn't give you a chance to answer. This irritated Slumber as well as Rags and Willie, but none of them did more than frown a little before they obeyed.

"Take your hands out your pockets and do what she says," Slumber told his brothers. "You can see well as me what we're up against. It's the best thing to let a girl like Daisy Bee have her own way."

The others seemed to agree. They had to let her teach them.

V

Eighth Avenue

THE next morning Uncle Jasper Tappin had his work to do, and he gave the boys jobs. To Willie and Slumber he gave mops and buckets and assigned a hall and a flight of stairs to each. When he got them started, he took Rags away and began teaching him to operate the service elevator.

If they were good, hard-working boys, he told them, they could help him a lot. It was a big job to keep a twelve-story apartment house clean from top to bottom. It required much help. Of course, there were always many boys and men who wanted jobs, but there were never enough of the ones who could be relied on to make a hall shine, who wouldn't leave fingerprints on the woodwork, and who would not sweep dirt into a corner and leave it there. Uncle Jasper Tappin wanted his nephews to know that he could well use three *good* helpers on his job, but that he might have to send them back home right away if they failed to do their work well That was about the way life was in a big city, he explained; people didn't have much patience. If you did your work to suit them, they'd employ you. If you did not, they'd let you go. They wouldn't waste many words talking about it. They could always find, and very easily too, somebody to take your place.

Slumber was impressed by these words. He put all his strength on the end of his mop handle and began talking to himself as he worked it back and forth on the white tile floor. His eyes sparkled, but his face became long and serious.

"Umpty-ump," he said, swinging his mop earnestly. "Umpty-ump and ump again. If you don't ump this time, I'll umpty you back again. Said, umpty this way and umpty that. Umpty-ump."

It was his own language, and if it didn't mean anything to anybody else, it meant a great deal to Slumber. What he meant to himself was that he was getting down to business and he didn't want any foolishness. He was going to

HE WAS GOING TO MAKE THOSE WHITE TILES SHINE OR ELSE SCRUB A HOLE IN THEM

make those white tiles shine or else scrub a hole in them. Those old tiles on that floor had just as well start smiling and looking pretty, because young papa Slumber was fixing to wash their faces. Yes, sir, young papa Slumber was fixing to wash their faces clean. That old hall had business to shine this morning.

Two or three hours later the service elevator stopped at the seventh floor where Slumber had been working and Rags and Uncle Jasper Tappin stepped out and walked down to the end of the hall where the mop bucket stood.

"Well, sir, how you making it, son?"

Slumber stood erect, rubbing his back to take the kink out.

"I been aiming to make things shine," he said softly.

"Well, that you done, let me tell you. I don't know when I last seen these tiles sparkling like all this," Uncle Jasper Tappin said.

"Them tiles is smiling because I washed their faces so good, that's what," Slumber told him.

"Oh, so that's what it is!" Uncle Jasper Tappin giggled. "I see right now that you going to be a big help to me. You done caught the secret about cleaning already. Make things smile — that's the ticket."

"How am I doing on that old service elevator?" Rags asked, because he was beginning to feel left out.

"Well, running a elevator is a little bit different, but never mind, I think you'll do."

"How Willie coming along?" Slumber asked.

"Well, Willie is just a little fellow, but he'll learn. We just took him down to the basement. You can come now, too. This one hall and stair is all you have to do today. Put your mop and bucket in the service elevator and we'll knock off for this morning. This evening I might want you to do something else for me."

They all went down to the basement together. Slumber put the mop and bucket away, and then went in and washed himself for lunch. While they were at the table, Uncle Jasper Tappin told the boys that they might go out in the afternoon and start seeing the sights. And since this was exactly the thing all of them had been waiting to hear him say, no one answered a word. He gave each of them a nickel, and immediately all three of the boys shoved their chairs back from the table and went into the bedroom for their caps.

Passing the table where their old uncle and aunt sat, each of the youngsters spoke politely, first Rags, then Willie, and finally Slumber.

"See you later, Uncle Jasper Tappin."

"Be back directly, Aunt Ludy."

"Look for me when you see me, you all both."

Slumber turned to close the door, and the two old people saw his long face, his round sad eyes, but they knew he was happier than he looked. They knew he could hardly wait to get out on the streets. For though the boys had seen the whole city from the roof, they were more anxious than ever to get a close view of things.

The boys walked to the entrance of the park at the corner and went down the long flight of stairs to the green lawns, the benches and the playgrounds. On some of the benches sat old men smoking. On others there were women watching the small tots who played on the walk. The playgrounds were filled with boys and girls, some of them as large as Rags and Slumber and Willie.

"We can come down here and play sometime," Willie suggested.

"Yes," Slumber said, "but not today. We got to do a heap of just plain looking before we can study about playing on them swings and things. This man's town is just full up with things to see."

"You tell him, Slumber, while I listen," Rags said without turning his head.

When they came to the end of the park, they turned toward the street above which the elevated cars passed. And in just a few moments Slumber's eyes were popping out almost like a frog's eyes. His mouth had dropped open, and he was doing some powerful looking. There before him was a row of pushcarts that continued down the street further than he could see. And each one was loaded with more kinds of fruits and foods and things to sell than three boys could shake a stick at.

There was one cart with oranges neatly arranged in a beautiful pyramid. Another one was loaded with lemons and grapefruit. Others had displays of apples. Then there were the vegetable carts, dozens and dozens of them, loaded with fine greens, cabbages, carrots, beets, green peas, Irish potatoes and summer squash. More oranges and apples followed, and vegetables till you couldn't rest. In between there were carts with plantains and mangoes and avocadoes and other fruits unfamiliar to Slumber and his brothers.

One man pushed a go-cart with an iron kettle of fire on it. He had roasted chestnuts to sell. Another one had a little oven on wheels in which he baked sweet potatoes and kept them warm for anyone who didn't have time to go home and cook. There were carts loaded with eggs, fresh from the country, and others that sold plates and dishes and pans for the kitchen. Still others had bolts of cloth and articles of clothing. And Slumber began to think that a person could buy almost anything he needed right there at those Eighth Avenue pushcarts.

Many housewives were on the Avenue with shopping bags on their arms, picking over the fruits and vegetables. On the corner a tall man in a preacher's coat and a silk hat stood eating the big warm sweet potato he had just bought. A little further down the block a milkman's horse was standing where he could slip his head over the top of a cart when the owner was not looking and help himself to a bunch of carrots or a head of lettuce. Maybe it was because the pushcart man felt sorry for the hungry horse that he kept looking the other way and pretended not to see while the animal enjoyed a really fine lunch.

But in spite of all the things he saw on the pushcarts, Slumber had not yet decided where he would spend his nickel. Surely he would *not* buy a baked sweet potato or any roasted chestnuts; he had too many of those at home in Alabama. The boys continued to walk. Then, suddenly, they came to a cart they could not pass. It was a cart loaded with nothing but neckties. Above it there was a large pasteboard sign which said *Bergman's Beautiful, Washable Neckties, 5¢ each.* On one side of the cart stood Mr. Bergman, a short man with whiskers and a derby hat. On the other side stood Mrs. Bergman. And on a stool in front sat their little son, Abie.

Slumber's hand ran to the collar of his own shirt. No, there was no necktie there. In fact,

Slumber had never owned a necktie. And to think, these were only 5 cents each! They were pretty, too — red, yellow and green and mixed colors. Slumber stood looking at them and turning his nickel in his hand.

"You like a nice new necktie?" Mr. Bergman asked, smiling.

"I'm just studying," Slumber said. "I always did like pretty neckties, but ——"

Slumber's voice broke off. He noticed something down in the next block that took his breath.

"But what?" Mr. Bergman asked. "Why don't you pick one out for yourself? How about this one, this yellow one with the stripes?"

"I see something down the street and I think somebody needs me," Slumber said. "I'll be back later."

Slumber and Rags and Willie started off on a run. And by now other folks had seen the commotion and were running the same way.

Two cooks wearing aprons and caps, two of the biggest and fattest cooks in Harlem, had picked up the same bunch of turnips, and now they couldn't seem to decide who had picked it up first. One was clinging to the tops, the other to the turnips, and they were pulling against each other with all their strength and talking very loudly as they pulled.

"It's mine; I had it first," cried one.

"No, it's mine," the other shouted. "I was holding it in my hand."

One pushcart man came running up and said it belonged to the cook with the heavy mustache. He said he was sure he had seen him pick up the bunch of turnips first. Another pushcart man left his cart full of apples and came running to say that he had seen the cook with the chin whiskers holding the bunch of turnips in his hand.

Then other pushcart men came running and joined in the noise. Everybody was shouting at the top of his voice by now. Two or three of the housewives got bumped so hard they dropped their shopping bags.

Slumber was so excited he couldn't speak. The boys had now decided not to come too near the crowd for fear one of them might get stepped on in the confusion. But Slumber did not like to see trouble. He wanted the cooks to stop quarreling and the pushcart men to go back to their own carts. What could he do? Oh, what could he do? Slumber was almost ready to cry. Should he run down there and bump into the crowd and make them stop that way? Should he shout at them? Well, neither of these seemed a good suggestion.

Without thinking, and before he knew what he was doing, he found his hands full of Irish potatoes. The next minute he was throwing them, throwing them hard, the way he threw at heifers in Alabama when he wanted to drive them out of the corn. Maybe that would stop them, he thought. Maybe they would forget about the bunch of turnips and try to find out where the potatoes were coming from.

And that was exactly what they did. One of the pushcart men took an orange from his cart and came running toward the boys, ready to throw it. Another one came with an apple. Another one picked up a coconut.

The boys saw the crowd coming. Just that quickly everybody had forgotten about the two angry cooks, and no doubt the cooks had forgotten about themselves.

"Now look what you done done," Rags said

suddenly. "See there, they're all coming at us."

"I reckon we better be leaving," Slumber murmured in a calm voice. "No need staying round here all day."

"I'm gone already, big bubber," Willie whispered, starting to run.

Slumber followed him.

"Me, too, son," he said.

"Well, you two little half-pints better pat a heap of pavement in the next few minutes if you don't want me to step on you, because I'm turning on the speed, me, and I don't aim to blow no horn," Rags told the others, coming up behind them with his long strides.

A moment later the boys turned a corner and began to feel a little safer. Slumber put his hand in his pocket and remembered his nickel. It began to look as if he would have to find another place to spend it. They couldn't possibly go back and buy one of those Bergman neckties now.

THE BOYS TURNED A CORNER AND BEGAN TO FEEL A LITTLE SAFER

VI

Harlem Boys

TWO or three days passed, and then came an afternoon on which the boys had nothing to do but sit in the park on a bench. For a while they flipped their nickels and played heads and tails, but finally Slumber thought of something that had been in his mind since the first day they reached New York.

"What's that down-under-the-ground car what they talk about so much?" he asked suddenly.

"The subway," Rags said. "That's the name they call it."

"How much you reckon it cost to take a ride on it?"

Rags's eyes brightened, and he wondered why none of them had thought of that question before.

"Dog my cats," he said, all excited. "You done thought up something grand, Slumber."

"What you talking about, big shorty?" Slumber said, puzzled.

"I'm talking about you and me and Willie taking a long ride on that subway train. It just cost a nickel to go there and come back."

"To go where?" Slumber asked, his face so long and sad it almost made his brothers laugh.

"To go where the subway take you," Rags told him.

But that explanation was just too much for little Willie's logical mind.

"Well, where in the nation do the subway *take* you?" he demanded.

Rags thought for a moment, then he shook his head and shrugged his shoulders.

"I don't know where the subway take you, and I ain't bothered," he said. "I reckon it take you anywhere you want to go, but just so long as it bring you back where you come from, I don't care where it go. Come on with me, you all. A subway ride is just the ticket for us."

Slumber and Willie did not answer, but their prompt response to Rags's suggestion was evidence enough of their agreement and pleasure. Rags took Willie's hand and commenced walking so fast the little fellow had to almost run to keep up. Slumber followed a few steps behind, his hands deep in his pockets, his head hanging sadly. Yet he felt far from sad this afternoon. Slumber was just thinking hard as he shuffled along behind his brothers. He was trying to imagine how a down-under-the-ground car looked and how it would feel to ride on one. But it didn't do any good to think about it. Slumber concluded that the subway train was one of those things you simply had to see.

They had walked three or four blocks when Rags and Willie paused at the top of the steps that led down to the underground tracks.

"Got your nickels ready?" Rags asked, looking first at Slumber, then at Willie.

"Here mine," Willie said, taking his from his pocket.

"I got mine," Slumber whispered.

They went down the steps slowly. All of the boys were puzzled by the strange lay-out of things in the subway station, so they took their time and noticed carefully what the other people did.

Slumber discovered that the small booth with the man sitting at the window was the place where people got their money changed. Then he noticed that the folks entering the trains had to first pass through one of the gates in front of the booth. These would allow only one person to enter at a time and would swing open only after the person had dropped a nickel in the slot at the side.

"Um-hunh," Slumber said aloud. "I got that old gate down pat. You puts your nickel in that there place yonder. Then you pushes that turn-around thing what looks like a wagon wheel with four spokes in it. When the wheel spin around, in you go. It's a mighty fine contraption, too, but I believe I can work it slick as a whistle."

"Well, you go first then," Rags said. "It ain't good to be so smart, you know."

"I ain't being smart," Slumber said, dropping his coin in the proper place. "I just got this old subway business down pat. Now, look at me. See there, I'm in. Now you come in."

Sure enough, Slumber was in. The thing that looked like a wagon wheel with four spokes made a big noise and turned just far enough to let Slumber through. Then it would not move any further until another coin was dropped into the slot.

"That was pretty slick how you went through there, bubber," Rags admitted. "Now watch me. Here I come."

Rags got through safely, but Slumber could see that the older boy's heart was in his mouth as he dropped the nickel in the slot. Perhaps, Slumber thought, Rags was wondering for just a moment whether or not the wheel would turn after it had his nickel safely in its box. But a moment later he saw a smile running across his brother's face. The wheel was turning.

Willie had watched it all carefully. Now it was his turn. Without saying a word and without dropping his nickel in the slot — without even trying to turn the wheel that let you in the gate — Willie just ducked his head and ran *under* the wheel. And there he was, inside with his brothers, laughing about what he had done and holding his coin up before them to show them what he had saved by ducking under the turn-wheel. But he did not laugh long. He did not hold his nickel up before Rags and Slumber very long. A big powerful man in a uniform came running and caught little Willie by the shoulder.

"Trying to come in without paying, hunh? Trying to steal a ride on the subway, are you? Well march yourself right out of here and come in right, if you come in at all."

The guard's voice was stern and just a little angry. But he did not wait for Willie to march *himself* out. The subway guard kept his hand on the boy's shoulder until the marching was over and Willie was out where he started from.

"Now come in right, if you want to," the guard repeated. "What do you think those turn-wheels are for?"

Willie then dropped his coin in the slot just as his brothers had done. And when he came through the gate this time he was not smiling, but he felt much better.

A train of ten cars came roaring through the dark tunnel under the ground, its two small lights shining like eyes. It stopped at the platform where the boys stood. All of the doors opened at once, and Slumber and Rags and Willie entered the one nearest them. Inside the car they found seats and sat trembling as it began to pull away.

Gradually the moving train gathered speed. Soon it was going almost as fast as lightning; and as it sped down there under the ground in its tunnel, the car was filled with a roaring noise. Slumber noticed that Rags was saying something, his mouth was moving, but the train made so much noise, Slumber couldn't hear a word he said.

The train came to other underground stations and at each stop people got on and off. All of them seemed to know where they were going. Some read newspapers as they rode. Somehow the subway seemed just like an ordinary every-day thing to them. But Slumber was so happy and excited and frightened and tickled he soon forgot about all the people who didn't know a good ride when they took one.

"Whee!" he cried, as the subway roared around a long sloping curve, reaching a terrific speed.

"I help you to say whee!" Willie squealed.

"Turn on the speed, Mr. Subway Man," Rags shouted. "I don't like nothing but fast trains, me."

Slumber stood up and tried walking in the moving car. It was hard to keep your feet at first, but it was fun. He motioned to Rags and Willie and they followed him through the car. They walked through car after car till they reached the open door at the very front of the train. There the wind was strong, but the boys enjoyed it because they could look ahead into the dark tunnel through which the tracks ran.

After a while the train came up out of the tunnel and ran on an elevated track above the streets.

"Well, now ain't this something," Slumber said. "This old train done come up out the ground—just when I was commencing to like it down there, too."

"Couldn't we get off and go back?" Willie asked.

"I reckon we going to have to get off and go back sometime soon. You can't keep going this way all the time."

"You talking sense, big shorty," Slumber said. "Let's get off next time the train stop and gc back again!"

At the next station the boys got off and went to the entrance gate.

"Now how we going to get over on the other side and catch one of them trains going back?" Rags said.

"Just go out this way," Slumber said, pushing the gate open and going through. "Then we can go downstairs and come up on that side over yonder."

Rags looked at Slumber and groaned.

"Look what you done gone and done, bubber. You ain't got the sense you was born with. Now look where you is. Just look at yourself."

Slumber couldn't see anything wrong with himself.

"I thought you wanted to go back the way we come," he said meekly.

"You crazy possum-head boy you," Rags shouted. "Don't you see you is outside and you can't come back in without another nickel. Now how you going to get back home?"

"Oh," Slumber said. "Oh . . ."

Tears were already in Willie's eyes.

"We going to leave Slumber here?" he asked Rags.

"I don't know what we going to do."

But there was no need to moan now. The

boys had traveled enough to know that you didn't get anywhere by standing still. You didn't go places by quarreling and grumbling.

"I'm got to get home, some kind of way," Slumber said simply.

"And I expect we best come the same way," Rags said, disgusted.

He and Willie pushed through the gates — they turned very easily when you were coming out — and followed the sad Slumber down the steps to the ground.

"I don't know where I'm at, and I don't know which way is home," Slumber murmured. "But if ever I get back to Harlem, I'll know more about traveling on that old subway train next time. That's a tricky old something-or-another-way they got them subway gates fixed up. You is just as apt to get yourself locked out as you is to get locked in."

They were walking down a paved highway, Slumber playing a tune on his harmonica, when a taxi cab stopped at the curb and honked at them.

"Say, ain't you all Harlem boys?" the cab driver called.

'NOW HOW YOU GOING TO GET BACK HOME?'

"Yes, *suh*," Slumber called back. "We sure is Harlem boys and we aiming to get back home the best way we can."

"Come on hop in then," the driver said. "I'm a Harlem taxi driver. I just happened to drive somebody way out this way, and I'd just as soon carry you three back with me as not."

"Much obliged," the boys said, getting into the cab. "We is sure proud to get a ride home."

"You say you're Harlem boys?"

"Well, suh," Slumber said, trying to explain a little better, "I was just beginning to think we was Harlem boys, but after what happened to us this afternoon, I kind of think we is still Alabama boys."

The cab driver laughed as they told him how Slumber had got off the subway and left the gate before noticing that it was not possible to come back in without another coin. He agreed with them that they were not really Harlem boys. But he thought that did not matter, because they all seemed to be very good-humored and amusing Alabama boys.

Night came while they were on the way home. All the street lights were on when the cab stopped in front of their home. Uncle Jasper Tappin was smoking a pipe in the basement entrance when he saw the cab door open and the boys get out. For a moment he thought he must have been dreaming.

The boys were giggling proudly as they met him. But Uncle Jasper Tappin could not imagine what had happened or how they could arrange to come home in such fine style.

"Dog my cats," he said, shaking his old head. "You three is the beatingest set of boys that ever I *did* see."

VII

The Library

THE next afternoon, when their work was done and they had eaten their lunch, the boys found their caps and started through the park again.

While they walked, Slumber thought of something.

"If Daisy Bee was here," he said, "she might could tell us where to go."

"She knows a lot," little Willie said, "but I'm glad she's not here. She makes me tired — knowing so much like she does."

"Maybe she could kept us out of that trouble on Eighth Avenue and on the subway," Rags said. "I wonder how come we don't see her any more."

"We might run across her sometime again," Slumber murmured.

"It's a good thing we didn't tell Uncle Jasper

Tappin about all that throwing you started the other day," Rags said, looking at Slumber.

"Yes," Slumber admitted, "it sure were a good thing we didn't tell him. He might of got mad."

"Like as not we'd be on our way home to Alabama now, if we had told on Slumber," Willie said.

Rags shook his finger in Slumber's face.

"And I want to tell you something else," he said. "Don't you start no such foolishment today like you did on them other days. Do, and I'm going to leave you standing up by yourself and let you take your own medicine. Me and Willie will go straight and tell Uncle Jasper Tappin."

"I don't aim to chunk no more," Slumber said.

"Well, make sure you don't," his brother told him.

Some time later, when they had walked about fifteen blocks and turned one corner, the boys found themselves in front of a building that interested them. The building had tall windows and large entrance doors; and as the boys stood on the pavement trying to make out what it was, they saw many boys and girls as well as older folks going in and coming out. And the very peculiar thing about these people was that nearly every one carried books into the building or else brought books out.

Slumber was overcome by curiosity. He put himself in front of a small boy coming down the steps and spoke to the youngster.

"What you all having inside here, son — school?"

The boy laughed.

"School's been closed a month," he said. "This the library."

Slumber wrinkled his forehead.

"How you call that name again, son?" he asked.

"The library — The Public Library."

Each of the boys seemed greatly puzzled. They were not sure they knew what the youngster meant by a library or a Public Library. Finally Slumber decided that the best thing to do was to pretend to know and then ask a few other questions.

"Oh," he said. "A library, hunh! Well,

ain't that fine. What they selling today — anything you can get for a nickel?"

"*Selling?*" the boy cried. "What you mean selling?"

Slumber knew he was not on the right track.

"I mean, do it cost anything to go in?"

"'Course not," the boy said, walking away. "Ain't you ever heard of a library before? Where you been all this time?"

Those words did not make the boys feel any more cheerful, but they made no answer.

"There's nothing like finding out," Rags suggested.

"You right," Slumber told him. "Let's go inside."

At the downstairs desk of the building there was a lady who told the boys that the children's department was on the second floor and that they would have to go upstairs. Slumber did not mind that. He followed Rags and Willie up the steps and came to the desk of another lady on the second floor.

"Do you boys want to draw some books?" she asked, as the three stood before her desk looking strange and lost.

All the boys shook their heads slowly.

"No'm," Slumber answered.

"Did you come for the story hour?" the lady smiled.

Again the boys shook their heads very slowly. And the sad look on Slumber's face became sadder than ever.

"No'm," he told her honestly. "We didn't come for no story hour. We ain't never heard nothing *about* no story hour."

By now the library lady was terribly puzzled. It did no good at all for her to ask the boys questions, so she decided to wait for them to tell her what they wanted. She had worked in a library a good many years, but the only things she had ever seen children come to the library for was to borrow books on their cards or else to hear the stories she told during the story hour. Sometimes, of course, they just sat and read, but that was generally while they were trying to select the books they wanted to take home to read.

Still the three boys stood before her desk and said nothing. Something would have to be done, she thought. They could not stand there all afternoon, looking at her so strangely. Soon there would be other youngsters coming to return books, and these boys would be standing in the way.

"Well, maybe you'd better come into the reading room here and look at some of the books," she said.

Slumber and his brothers really had no idea what they wanted to do; in fact, they had no idea what they were supposed to do in a library, but they were polite boys and they were all anxious to do whatever was right in such a strange big place.

"Yes'm," Slumber said, speaking for his brothers as well as himself, "that'll be just the ticket."

"Of course, boys, you understand this room is to be kept quiet for reading. You must subdue your voices and make no disturbance," the librarian explained kindly.

"Yes'm," the boys murmured, a little uncertain.

She put books that she thought would amuse them into their hands, and immediately all three settled down at the little tables and began poring over the pictures. The lady went back to her desk.

A few moments passed quietly. Then, for some reason, Slumber's eyes began to sparkle. A moment later there was a smile on his sad face; his teeth began to show. Presently he was giggling out loud.

"What in the nation is eating on Slumber?" little Willie asked Rags. "Don't know when I last saw him giggling and carrying on like all that."

"Laughing bug must be biting him," Rags said.

They began looking at their own books again, and for a time it seemed that Slumber would settle down and get quiet again. But before they could turn more than two or three pages, Slumber dropped his book and burst into a big laugh that could be heard all through the library.

"Oo — wee!" he cried. "Look at him go! Hee-hee-hee! He's an old gingerbread man, and see there, he's done hopped out of the oven and started down the street. Oo-wee! Go it, Mister Gingerbread Man!"

The other boys left their books and came running to see Slumber's gingerbread man that hopped out of the oven and ran down the street.

Sure enough, there it was just as Slumber told it. Little Willie and Rags burst into loud laughter too. These library books were simply wonderful. Wouldn't it be grand if real gingerbread cakes like their mama made would jump out of the oven and cut-up like that sometimes.

"That gingerbread man beats the band," Willie cried. "Let's take it home and show Uncle Jasper Tappin and Aunt Ludy and Daisy Bee."

But while they were laughing and enjoying the picture and thinking about taking it home to show their uncle and aunt and Daisy Bee, they looked up into the face of the library lady again. They had not seen her come and they had not heard her footsteps, but there she was looking down upon them very sternly.

"Boys," she said, "this is the public library. We can't have noise in here. Others are trying to read. Maybe you had better go home. I'll take your books."

They handed them to her sadly. They bowed their heads sorrowfully and started toward the stairs. Slumber heard the lady's words going round and round in his mind. *Boys, this is the public library. We can't have noise in here.*

Well, he had not meant to do wrong. In fact, he had forgotten all about being in the library. That gingerbread man — oh, sakes-alive, that thing was a cut-up for true. But it was just too terrible to have to leave the library now, just when the books were becoming interesting.

They went out the big door downstairs.

"It's all your fault, Slumber," Willie said. "You shouldn't of called us to look at that gingerbread man."

"I didn't go to do it," Slumber said. "I was just tickled."

"You always get us in trouble, you do," Rags said. "I don't believe you got good sense."

Slumber did not mind Rags's words so much because brothers can sometimes say extremely cruel things to each other without hurting very badly, but a sorrowful look was coming over his face just the same.

"You not fixing to cry, is you?" little Willie asked.

Slumber did not answer. He simply put his hands into his pockets and walked between his brothers. He was busy talking to himself in his mind, and this is what he was saying: One these days I'm coming back to this library and look at that book some more. I'm going to look at the rest of them books too, but I ain't going to laugh out loud, and I'm not going to call nobody else to come look neither. And when I go home to Alabama, I'm going to tell my mama what I looked at, too.

"Why don't you say something?" Rags asked after a while.

"I'm too busy studying," Slumber told him. "I got a heap of things to think about."

VIII

"Now Guess Where I'm Going"

DURING the next few days Slumber was careful to get his brothers into no more trouble. The three worked hard, helping Uncle Jasper Tappin clean the halls every morning; and often in the afternoon the uncle found something for them to do in the basement. There was always plenty of work to do in a big apartment house, and it had always to be done in a big hurry. But work was like play to Slumber and his brothers; they were used to it.

One afternoon, when they were playing handball behind the building, the boys heard a window open a few floors up, and a moment later they saw Daisy Bee's face and heard her calling them from the apartment in which she lived.

"Hello, you lazy-bones, you."

Slumber looked at his two brothers, and they looked at him. Then he turned his face upward and called back, "What's that name you calling us, Daisy Bee?"

She laughed at him.

"Nothing. But why don't you do your work?"

"We done did our work," he said proudly.

"Well, that's different," she said. "How would you all like to go somewheres?"

"Fine," Willie called. "Where you going?"

"I'll give each one of you one chance," she said, "and if you guess where I'm getting ready to go, you can go with me — hear?"

"I know," Rags said. "You're going to the park to play."

"Wrong," Daisy Bee told him. "You guess, Willie."

"You getting ready to go to the library."

"No, you're wrong too. You guess, Slumber."

"I guess you fixing to go see the parade," he said.

"You guessed it, sad-faced boy," Daisy Bee called. "You better go out in the front and wait now, because I'll be coming down directly."

"Son, you a powerful good guesser," Rags said to Slumber, after Daisy Bee had left the window. "How'd you think up that good guess?"

"I heard some talk about a parade," Slumber said sadly.

"Slumber is powerfully smart sometimes, ain't he, Rags?" Willie said.

"You said it right, bubber. He smart sometimes, and this here is one of them *sometimes*."

"We better go out front if we don't want to get left," Willie suggested.

Slumber put the handball in his pocket, and they went through the basement to get their caps and to tell Uncle Jasper Tappin and Aunt Ludy where they were going.

When the four met in front of the building, they wasted no time.

"We'd better hurry. I don't know just when the parade will start passing."

That suited the boys. They walked rapidly through the park and down the cross street to the Avenue. It took them only a few minutes, but they were nearly out of breath when they reached the place. The street was lined with people, but the parade had not yet started. In fact, it was not even in sight, and the youngsters had time to walk up and down the Avenue a little while, looking at things and trying to pick out the best spot from which to watch the parade when it came.

And that day there was indeed a great deal to see on the Avenue. People were dressed in their best clothes, because it was Sunday afternoon and all the churches were out. Slumber looked at everyone he passed and tried to pick out the clothes he liked the best.

One man, who impressed him very much, had on a checkered suit and a bow tie that looked like a big butterfly. There was a young woman whose feet looked like little canary birds in her pretty yellow slippers. An older woman had on a hat that suggested a Guinea hen. A very small man wore a frock-tailed coat that reached his ankles and a stovepipe hat that kept slipping down over his ears. All the men had shiny shoes and wore well-pressed suits. All the women wore high-heeled shoes and dresses that had been freshly washed and ironed. A good many of the clothes looked brand new to Slumber.

Oh, it was impossible to decide which clothes he liked best. Slumber gave up trying.

Suddenly, as the three boys and Daisy Bee

walked behind the rows of people who lined the curbstone, they saw something that made them draw back with fear. Two immense yellowish dogs were coming toward them on the sidewalk. The animals were nearly as large as lions; and as they came down the street, they pulled on their chains so hard they nearly upset the small man who tried to keep them in check.

"Oo-wee!" Willie cried. "Did you ever see or hear tell of such big old dogs?"

"I never did," Slumber murmured, "and I'm mighty sorry I had to come here and see these. I believe I'd rather look at a grizzly bear than to look at them two uglies coming yonder."

At every few steps the dogs would rise up on their hind legs, and you could see then that they were much taller than any man. And the worst thing about them was that they never smiled. If they showed their teeth at all, it was only to growl and frighten people. The big coon dogs that Slumber had seen in Alabama would have looked like young puppies beside these two creatures, and the boy began to wonder why anybody would ever want to make friends with anything so big and terrible.

"You look like you're getting ready to run," Daisy Bee said, looking at Slumber.

"Don't say a word," Slumber answered honestly. "I'm apt to leave here if you just talk too loud. Looking at them two big scamps makes me think about traveling."

"Don't run," Daisy Bee said. "Just stand way over here while they pass. I've seen them before, and they never bother anybody. They are Great Danes."

The boys looked at each other curiously. Then, beginning with Slumber, each one said slowly, "Oh, I see." The words were whispered very softly, and it may have been that the boys were still afraid, but after that they didn't let on.

Slumber closed his eyes when the dogs were directly in front of them, so he did not see when they actually passed. With his eyes closed, he managed to keep walking by holding Rags's sleeve. At the same time he was able to keep himself from running or jumping or crying, and nobody other than himself ever knew how afraid he was.

The four youngsters walked to another corner and looked down the street again. Still the parade was nowhere near. Daisy Bee remembered that a man called a Human Fly was going to climb a building just before the parade, and she thought they would have time to watch him if they hurried.

The building was one of the tallest in that part of New York. It was located where two prominent streets crossed, and already there was such a crowd of people standing around it, the youngsters could scarcely worm their way through the crowd. And when they finally did reach a place where they could see, the Human Fly was already more than half-way up the building. He was climbing on the outside, not like a fly climbs, but more like a monkey, catching the ledge of bricks at each window and pulling himself up till he could reach inside the window and take a firmer hold. It gave Slumber the creeps to see a man playing around on the outside of a tall building like that. He imagined how he would feel if he had to just sit in those high windows and wash the panes. Why, if Uncle Jasper Tappin gave him any such job as that, Slumber would just have to disappoint the old man. Before he realized it, Slumber was so absorbed in what he saw that he began talking aloud to himself.

"Well, peoples!" he said. "I might don't know nothing much, but I got better sense than to do that. That there is just natural born craziness. Look at him there now, hanging out there by his one hand. I wonder do anybody put him up to do that foolishness."

"He gets money for it," Daisy Bee said. "People will do anything for pay."

"What people!" the boys cried. "What people you talking about, Daisy Bee? Not none of us three — you don't mean us."

They all laughed.

"I mean some people will do most anything you tell them to do if you pay them enough."

"Well, I call that craziness," Slumber repeated.

After the Human Fly reached the top, the people began to scatter. The youngsters could see the parade coming away down the Avenue, so they decided to find a good place and wait. They could hear the music very distinctly. Slumber loved music more than almost anything, and the horns and drums made his heart beat fast.

He began talking in his mind to himself, Come on down the line, mister drum-beating man. Come on, you horn-blowers, too. Come along, all.

All the people began to cheer. Slumber could hardly keep still.

IX

The Parade

AT the head of the parade walked a man tall enough to sit on top of an automobile. He was a very thin man, about the size of the men on the street, but his legs were terribly long. He walked proudly ahead of the procession of decorated cars, and every once in a while he'd step out of line and take a little rest sitting on the top of a truck. Once he stepped up on the sidewalk and leaned his elbow on a second floor window sill. Another time he shook hands with some people who were leaning out of their windows to look at the parade. Then, when he saw that the rest of the parade was about to catch up with him, he went back to the middle of the street and began marching again.

"Oo-wee!" Slumber cried. "Look at that big old man. How you reckon he got way up there like that?"

"He must eat a lot," Willie said.

"Eating a lot wouldn't make anybody grow that tall," Rags said.

Daisy Bee laughed at the boys.

"Don't you know what makes him so tall? He's got stilts on."

"No, he ain't," Slumber said.

"Yes, he has," she said. "They're under his pant legs. You just can't see them."

Slumber shook his head. He was not sure that Daisy Bee knew what she was talking about this time. The man had on ordinary shoes, and Slumber had never seen any stilts with shoes on them. He wasn't a bit sure. That man was just natural born tall, he believed. But there was no more time to think about it now. Other things were coming down the street.

There were first the decorated cars in which rode men in black suits and black stovepipe hats. Then came a band. The men in the band were dressed in fancy uniforms with big bright buttons, and their leader walked ahead of them with a tall funny hat on his head. He carried a long gold stick with a ball on one end, and as he marched and led his band, he spun this stick around in the air. He made fancy steps, too, almost dancing to the music.

Then there were people marching, men in white suits and straw hats, carrying walking canes. They were followed by another band in a different kind of suits. And after the band there came an old mashed-up car in which two clowns rode. Whenever this car ran a short distance, it would turn up on its hind wheels, and one of the funny old men in it would get thrown out. The boys and Daisy Bee laughed hard at this.

A little later two more funny men came by. One of them was leading a very peculiar horse, and the other was walking behind the horse and trying to keep the animal moving. That old horse was a case, for sure. He seemed to be almost empty inside, and once or twice it looked as if he would break down in the middle. But the worst thing about that horse was that every now and then he would show his teeth and grin like a silly old person. He would sometimes stop and cross his legs, too. And the more the two men tried to make him behave, the more foolishness he carried on.

"I wouldn't have no such a old horse as that," Willie said.

"Shucks," Slumber said. "I wouldn't give five cents for that thing. That old horse is just making a monkey out of hisself."

"He sure is sway-backed and raw-bony a plenty," Rags said.

"He ain't a real horse, you know," Daisy Bee said. "Look at them feet."

Sure enough, the animal had feet as big as a man, and he wasn't even a large horse.

"Well, I reckon he ain't," Slumber said, "but whatever he is, he is sure acting a monkey. Look a yonder now, his back legs sitting down and his front legs standing up."

A moment later one of the men lit a cigar and put it in the horse's mouth to make him get up and keep marching. This seemed to please the old critter, and he walked along quite nicely as he puffed on his cigar.

"No," Rags said, "he sure ain't a real horse."

By that time there was another band coming. Some men in black suits followed this time. Then came women in white dresses. There were a good many flags and banners flying. And finally, after more bands and more people marching, the last band came along. Behind it walked people who did not seem to belong in the parade because they were not dressed in uniform of any kind and they did not march orderly or in line.

"We can march in it, too," Daisy Bee said. "You boys want to?"

They all said sure, and the four fell in behind the last band.

Just in front of them were two men carrying banners.

"This is fine," Slumber said softly. "This is what I been wanting to do for a long time."

The men of the band were tired and hot. Slumber noticed that the man beating the drum was limping. There was a scowl on his face. So the boy pushed his way up to the drummer and touched him on the sleeve.

"What you pecking at my sleeve for?" the drummer said, turning angrily.

"Nothing, mister," Slumber said. "You just look kind of tired. I was going to ask you does you want me to beat that drum for you."

"Aw, you can't beat this big old drum, son."

"How come?" Slumber said, keeping at his heels.

"Cause you got to have a uniform on to beat this drum. You got to wear these tight boots and this hot coat. That's why I'm having such a hard time."

"I can do that," Slumber said. "I'll do that for you."

The man stopped suddenly.

"You mean it, boy? You mean it for true?"

"Yes," Slumber said. And he stopped at once and began taking off his shoes.

The man was so happy to be rid of the tight shoes and the hot coat that his face was covered with smiles. He helped Slumber get into the things and handed Slumber's other shoes to Rags. It took only a moment, and before anybody else could tell what was happening, Slumber was marching with the band and pounding the big old drum for all he was worth. The shoes were too big and hard to walk in, but that did not matter now; Slumber was too happy to think about them. Neither did he mind the heavy drummer's coat that reached almost to his feet.

A moment later the man came running with

something he had forgotten to give Slumber. It was the drummer's cap. He slapped it down on Slumber's head, then ran away again. He was so glad to get those tight shoes off his feet and so anxious to get home that he bumped into people on the street.

The march was long and the day was hot, but the children did not mind. And before it was over, Daisy Bee was walking beside the leader of the band and making him let her swing his long gold stick.

"I reckon she up there showing him how he need to direct this band," Rags said, walking behind Slumber and carrying the shoes.

"That's about what she's doing," Willie said.

By and by, the two men carrying banners got tired and gave their jobs to Willie and Rags while they sat down on the curbstone to rest. But while the men were resting, the parade left them behind, and Willie and Rags got to carry the banners till the parade came to its end about an hour later.

There was a plenty to see and a plenty to hear as they marched along the streets of Harlem that afternoon, but the loudest thing any of them heard was Slumber beating that old drum with all his might. The prettiest thing they saw was Daisy Bee swinging that band leader's gold stick and showing the band man how to cut fancy steps in front of his band.

X

The Dozier Brothers

THE days grew hotter and hotter after the parade. A great many men came out on the streets of Harlem with little white wagons and sold water ices to the children. And it was not long before Slumber and Rags and Willie had spent all the nickels that Uncle Jasper Tappin could afford to give them. Then when the nickels were all gone, they found themselves still thirsty for water ices, and the days were still hot. Where would they get more nickels for water ices?

Slumber worried a great deal during the long afternoons. Harlem was surely no place to be without money. Harlem made you want things you never wanted before — like water ices and Eskimo pies and popsicles — but it didn't help you to get the money to buy these things. Slumber began to wish again that he were at home with his mama.

"If I was back home," he told Willie and Rags as they stood against the iron fence, looking down into the park, "I wouldn't be wanting no water ices or nothing like that. I wouldn't be studying about nothing such like. I'd just be chewing on a stalk of sorghum and feeling good."

"No, you wouldn't be feeling good," Rags said. "You going to always be wanting what you seen up here in Harlem. Even when you get back home again, you'll be wishing you had some popsicles. Once you start in wanting things, you can't never get over it. You shouldn't of come to Harlem."

"I reckon I shouldn't, but I want to go home just the same," Slumber said softly.

He did not fully agree with Rags about how he would keep on wanting the things he had seen in Harlem, even when he was home again. No, Slumber felt quite sure that when he reached home again, stretched himself out on the shady side of the house, scratched his bare feet in the cool ground and started chewing his stalk of sorghum cane, he would forget all about Eskimo pies and water ices and popsicles. But, of course, they were now a long way from home, and Uncle Jasper Tappin didn't seem to be in any special hurry to carry them back.

Slumber tried crossing his fingers and making wishes, but he found that nothing like that would work in Harlem. Those good luck tricks worked very well when he was at home in Alabama and in the country, but they didn't do a bit of good in New York. He found that in the big city to which he and his brothers had come even a rusty bent horseshoe or a rabbit's left hind foot wouldn't help you to get a cool water ice when you didn't have the nickel.

Little Willie finally thought of a wise thing. While they stood there, looking sorrowfully down into the park, he touched Rags on the back and said, "Listen, big shorty. I know what."

"What you know, little half-pint?" his brother said, smiling.

"Let's us go play some music and forget about what we has and what we hasn't got."

Slumber snapped his fingers, mocking his Uncle Jasper Tappin.

"Dog my cats," he said. "That's just the ticket."

So they went across the street and down into the furnace room where they did most of their playing nowadays. And there was no question about it — playing music did help a great deal.

That night when they were in bed, Slumber opened his eyes suddenly with a bright thought.

"Let's us start a band and call it the *Dozier Brothers Band,*" he said.

"Start a band with what?" Rags asked. "Just your harmonica and a tin can and a washboard?"

"Sure," Slumber said. "We can start with that and then look around and see what else we can find. Maybe Uncle Jasper Tappin will let you use that old guitar he got hanging on the wall."

Rags did not answer. The next afternoon, however, when their cleaning was done, he began to look around. Slumber kept his eyes open, too, and his thoughts were busy all morning.

"I seen some folks come in the air shaft with a old no-account band and play till people commenced throwing money at them from out the windows," he told Rags once. "We might could get us some nickels like how they did."

Rags was interested, but he was a little uncertain about the instruments. He wouldn't be satisfied with just a washboard to play on, and he was almost afraid to ask Uncle Jasper Tappin to let him take the guitar from off the wall. Yet, when the work was done, he made up his mind to try his luck.

In the meantime Willie found a broken drum in an ash can. Slumber repaired the old thing and painted the name of the band in big letters, *Dozier Brothers.* He struck the instrument a few strong booms, then handed it to his little brother.

"There now," he said. "You and me is fixed. If Rags will go ask Uncle Jasper Tappin for his guitar, we'll be ready for business."

Rags left the others in the furnace room and went to see about the instrument. While he was gone, Slumber and Willie went over a song or two, Slumber playing the tune on his harmonica and Willie beating the heavy part on the drum.

"How it sound?" Willie asked.

"Not so bad," Slumber said. "Not so bad."

About that time Rags came running through the door.

"Here it is, bubbers. Here it is," he cried. "Now we's *ready*."

"I told you so, big shorty," Slumber said, trembling with joy. "I told you he might would let you use it."

"He say it wasn't doing nobody no good up on the wall, cause he never yet seen a guitar what was made to be looked at. This old box was made for music, and here it comes. You listen."

Rags tuned the strings. Then, when Slumber began another song on his harmonica, he began to chime in with chords that sounded mighty fine indeed. Little Willie kept the drum booming just right. And the more they played, the sweeter the music sounded. The old furnace room had never heard anything like it.

No, sir, not since the building was built had there ever been music such as that in the furnace room. Slumber got warmed up and commenced to bear down on his harmonica. And when Slumber was warmed up, mind you, he could play a harmonica like very few people can play one. Why the little old furnace room windows started quivering and rattling to the tune.

Uncle Jasper Tappin's old coal shovel caught one of the notes and began humming it almost as if it had been struck by Willie's drum stick. Slumber was bearing down, and his brothers were keeping right with him.

"This coming Sunday we can get out and let the folks hear us," Slumber decided. "Soon in the morning, just about time they's getting out of bed good, they'll hear us down in the air shaft. Maybe they'll throw some money at us."

"Sometimes you think up some powerful smart things, Slumber," Willie said.

"He sure do," Rags said. "I don't see how he can do it and still be so dumb."

A smile came over Slumber's sad face.

"Sunday," he reminded the other two as they left the furnace room. "Sunday — soon in the morning."

XI

Bright Lights

DAISY BEE was sitting by the window reading a funny paper when she heard music down in the air shaft, far below. She stopped reading to listen, but at first she did not look out because it was nothing new to hear poor musicians playing down in the air shaft on Sunday morning. So many of them came that sometimes, when she was busy doing something else, Daisy Bee didn't even bother to open the window and look down, much less toss the players a penny. But today the music was not the same. It reminded her of something she had heard before, and she turned her ear to hear it better.

Yes, she thought, that was sweet playing down there in the air shaft. But that tune — where had she heard it before? Suddenly she remembered a tall country boy dancing lazily, another one beating on a tin can drum, and still another

— a sad-faced boy, this third one — playing a harmonica. Then she knew. It was the tune the boys had been playing on the roof the day she saw them first, and she remembered that Slumber had called it something about three country boys in a big city. It was just a kind of tune he made up in his head. But it was a very good tune, even if it was rather sad, and today it sounded much better than usual.

Daisy Bee opened a window and looked down. And there they were: little Willie beating the big drum they had found in an ash can, Rags whipping out chords on Uncle Jasper Tappin's box (or guitar, as some folks call it), and Slumber, the sad-faced boy, patting his foot and making the tune on that harmonica of his. They were a great set of boys, especially that Slumber, and Daisy Bee was glad to see that other windows were coming open and a few folks were tossing down coins wrapped in little scraps of newspaper.

The boys played two or three pieces, picked up their coins and then left to try their music on the people of some other building. So it was afternoon when Daisy Bee saw them again, and by that time they were hungry and pretty well tired out.

"I heard you playing this morning," she said, as the little troop reached the basement entrance with their large instruments.

"Was you listening, Daisy Bee?" Slumber said eagerly.

"Indeed I was," she told him again. "It sounded right good, too."

That pleased the three more than even the pennies and nickels in their pockets, because Daisy Bee was not one to praise what you did very readily. In fact, the boys were quite certain that she had told the band master in the parade just what was wrong with his band, and Rags and Willie remembered that at one time she had criticised them rather sharply for the way they played and danced. Daisy Bee was hard to please, and this was the first time the boys had ever received such a compliment from her.

"That's a mighty nice thing to hear you say," Slumber murmured timidly. "We aim to practice up this week so we can play some more good songs next Sunday."

The boys carried their instruments down to the basement apartment. After dinner they came up and sat on one of the benches looking down into the park. That afternoon they had money enough for all the Eskimo pies and popsicles and water ices and snowballs they wanted.

Daisy Bee, whose father and mother had a car, came downstairs wearing a very pretty new dress and drove away with her parents. But Slumber and his brothers did not forget what she had said to encourage them, and they began to think that playing in a band of your own like theirs was just about the best fun yet.

"Tomorrow we got to practice up good," Slumber said, licking his strawberry flavored snowball.

"You took the words out of my mouth," Rags said. "I was just fixing to say the same thing." He threw away the stick of his third popsicle.

Little Willie had just started on another cup of water ice, so he didn't say anything. But his brothers knew how he loved to beat that big drum, especially since they had painted the words *Dozier Brothers* on it.

The week passed slowly, but when next Sunday morning came, the band was even more successful than it had been the first time. They got more coins, and more people praised them.

This time it was Uncle Jasper Tappin who said, "Too bad Sunday don't come but once a week. You boys is doing pretty well with that band of yours."

"Yes," Slumber answered sadly, "too bad Sunday just come around now and then. I wish it was every day."

"Seem like you ought to could find somewheres to play on week days," Uncle Jasper Tappin said.

The boys wished it were true, but they had no idea where to go. That afternoon, however, they told Daisy Bee what Uncle Jasper Tappin had said and asked her what she thought about it.

"Sure, I know," she said. "Downtown is the place. I can't go because it'll be night, but mind where I tell you to go and you'll find the place all right. You'll make a lot of nickels, too."

Daisy Bee gave them the directions carefully. Rags wrote some of the words on a scrap of paper and put it in his pocket.

"That sound good, what you say, Daisy Bee," Slumber said.

They hurried downstairs and began getting their instruments in shape. Then, just as twilight was coming to the park, they caught an elevated train at the 155th street station.

"I don't know where we going," little Willie said, struggling to keep his drum out of the aisle, "but I know we on our way."

"Just don't let nobody step on that drum," Rags said. "We'll get there if the train keeps on running."

In the heart of New York there is the street of bright lights. Down there in that part of the city you walk between the rows of skyscraper buildings as the Indians used to walk between the walls of narrow canyons. You pass beneath the shadows overhead as the black men of the jungle used to pass beneath the trees of Africa. And you feel afraid sometimes when you walk there at night, just as the brave red men were sometimes afraid when they stood in the tall rocky canyons — just as the beautiful jungle men sometimes trembled in the shadows of their trees. But at night, when all those lights are burning, you almost forget the tallness of the buildings and the other things that make you afraid. You even forget sometimes how empty and dark the buildings are and what frightful black shadows they make.

The reason for the lights is that at that hour people are all going to theaters and concerts and places of amusement. Daisy Bee had explained this to the boys, and they were not disappointed. They walked to a place on the side street to which she had directed them. At first they wouldn't find anyone there, she had said, but they were to wait. By and by their time would come. The only trouble was that there was so much to look at as they went along and that people hurrying to be on time to their theaters nearly walked over the three youngsters.

The boys found their place in an alley behind a theater, and sat down to wait, and in less than an hour their time came. The side doors of the theater were flung open, and out came great crowds of people in evening clothes. It was the time of the intermission, and all the people were eager for a breath of fresh air and a chance to smoke a cigarette.

"Here we be," Slumber whispered to his brothers. "This is the time. Let's strike it up, big shorty."

Slumber drew the harmonica across his mouth. Rags whipped out the chords. Little Willie caught the time and began beating the drum. The theater people seemed delighted. They drew around the boys, forming a half circle. Slumber pulled his cap around sidewise, patted his foot and bore down on that lonesome railroad track tune of his: *Oh, blow your whistle on the Dixie Line.*

There was time for just two songs. Then a buzzer rang, and the people had to return for the rest of their program inside. But before they went away, they sprinkled the ground around the boys' feet with nickels and dimes and a few quarters.

Slumber was so excited he could not speak, but he helped his brothers to search well and make sure they had not overlooked a single coin. Then he said, "Well, I reckon we got them all."

"Yes, I reckon so," Rags agreed. "Now we going over to another theater in time for the

'THIS IS THE TIME. LET'S STRIKE IT UP, BIG SHORTY'

next intermission. That's how Daisy Bee said do."

At the second theater they succeeded just as well. A happy, surprised look came over the people's faces as they discovered the poorly dressed boys in the alley. Hearing the music, one man said, "This is a better show than the one inside," and he threw down a dollar bill.

"Now," Slumber said, still scarcely able to talk, "we got something to talk *about*."

"Yes," Rags said, "but you is so tickled and glad you can't keep from stuttering, and nobody won't *know* what you talking about."

"Let's hurry and get on the car before the theaters turn out," Willie suggested. "It's hard to carry this big old drum in a crowd."

The other boys thought that was sensible, so Slumber took one end of the instrument, and they hurried to the station.

XII

Abie

SOME things are simply too much fun to be true. Or if they are true, they are too good to last. That must have been the trouble with the Dozier Brothers Band. After just a few days of success something had to happen.

It was on a Thursday morning that little Willie woke up with a headache and a parched mouth. Aunt Ludy came into the room and felt his forehead. A few minutes later, when Slumber and Rags came in for breakfast, she said, "You all will have to eat without Willie this morning."

"How come that?" Slumber asked.

She shook her head slowly.

"Willie is feeling poorly today, son. He got considerable temperature, too."

"Sick, hunh?" Rags said.

"Sick," Aunt Ludy agreed, still shaking her head. "He is apt to be in bed two-three days, too."

Rags and Slumber agreed that this was bad news, powerful bad. And each one of them began to lose his appetite and to allow that he didn't feel at all hungry just yet.

"We want to go out in the furnace room a minute, Aunt Ludy," Slumber said. "Don't save us no breakfast."

That did not please Aunt Ludy, because she always thought folks should eat, after she had gone to the trouble to cook for them, but she did not object. Slumber's face was so long and sad she knew that he was greatly troubled.

When the boys reached the furnace room, they talked freely.

"What we going to do?" Slumber asked.

"That's just what I was fixing to ask *you*," Rags said.

They were talking about their band, of course. What was to become of the Dozier Brothers Band now that its drummer was sick? They had been having such good times and earning so many coins, they simply couldn't bear to think of giving up the business now.

"Little bubber be sick two-three days," Slumber said sadly. "Maybe more than that."

"The band can't stop," Rags said with determination.

"No," Slumber echoed weakly, "the band can't stop, but what we going to do for a drummer?"

"How about Daisy Bee?"

That was a bright notion. Why not try Daisy Bee? She could beat more drum in a minute than little Willie could beat in an hour. Why not ask her to join the Dozier Brothers?

It was afternoon when they saw Daisy Bee. She was coming out the front door with her skates, and when Slumber told her how things stood with them and what they expected of her, she shook her head.

"I could play the drum for you all here, but I can't go down town tonight. I always have to come in the house before dark," she said. "I can't stay up late neither."

So again Slumber and Rags were sorrowful. They began to feel that everything was lost and that there was nothing to do about it. Slumber turned his back to Daisy Bee so that she could not see the tears coming into his eyes.

"The band is all broke up," Rags said pitifully.

"How come?" Daisy Bee answered quickly. "Lots of boys in Harlem can beat a drum. Why don't you get one of them to help you out till Willie gets well?"

That was worth considering.

"Who could we get?" Rags asked.

"Send Slumber," she said. "He could find somebody."

It was agreed, and Rags returned to his work while Daisy Bee joined a group of children skating on the sidewalk. Slumber started through the park, walking slowly and showing with every step that he scarcely expected to succeed. Still he meant to do his best and to find a drummer to take Willie's place if it was at all possible.

An hour passed. Rags finished his work for the day. Another hour passed, and Rags went to the furnace room to plunk a few chords on the guitar and wait. Then, when he was just about to give up hope, he heard two boys coming toward the furnace room. For some reason, they seemed to be scuffling as they came, so Rags ran to meet them.

Just outside the door he saw Slumber dragging a small, pale child by the coat collar.

"What you doing to that boy?" Rags called.

"He wouldn't come," Slumber answered sadly. "I had to drag him all the way."

That Slumber was a case, Rags thought. There he had gone off and snatched somebody's boy by the collar and dragged him here to play the drum. But Slumber had made a terrible blunder. He had forgotten that this band was called the Dozier Brothers, and he had brought a boy who looked nothing like a Dozier Brother.

"I don't want to beat a drum," the new child cried. "I want to go back to my mama."

"Why didn't you get somebody that wanted to come?" Rags asked.

Slumber shook his head.

"I couldn't find none," he said. "This boy'll do, won't he?"

It was always rather dark in the basement, and today Rags couldn't see the boy very clearly, but still he doubted that they could use this youngster.

"He don't look like a Dozier Brother," he said.

"I thought about that," Slumber murmured. "I see what you mean. But maybe we could fix him up with shoe polish and make him look like us."

"What's your name?" Rags asked the boy, who had now stopped struggling.

"Abie," the boy said. "Abie Bergman."

"Oh, I know," Rags said. "Your papa is the necktie man."

Abie nodded.

"I was playing handball around the corner," little Abie said, "and he caught me and pulled me up here."

"We need you to beat the drum in our band," Slumber said. "I keep telling you that. We got to have somebody. You say you can beat a drum, and I don't see how come you don't come along and beat this one."

Abie didn't answer, so the boys led him into the furnace room and put a drum stick in his hand. Then Slumber drew the harmonica across his lips and began limbering up a tune. Rags tuned his box and struck a few chords.

"Now let's hear something from you, big shorty," Rags said to the little fellow.

Abie seemed to be feeling a trifle better. He caught the time and began beating the drum.

There was no doubt that he could beat a drum, and now that Slumber was commencing to bear down on the tune, he seemed very pleased to have a part in the music. Soon he had a smile on his face.

Of course, Slumber's harmonica playing would make almost anybody feel better, but it was wonderful how it changed Abie.

The next thing he said was, "Do you think that shoe polish will get in my eyes?"

"We'll keep it out of your eyes," Rags said.

It was about that time that Uncle Jasper Tappin came into the furnace room.

"I see you got a new drummer," he said.

"Yes, sir," Slumber said.

Then Slumber explained how he had found Abie and persuaded him to join their band. He also explained how he and Rags proposed to make the boy look like a Dozier Brother. But Uncle Jasper Tappin listened to it all, down to the very end, then shook his head.

"You done kidnapped that boy," he said. "You better take him back to his mama — and that right quick."

"But I don't want to go," Abie said bravely. "I want to go down town with the band."

Still Uncle Jasper Tappin shook his head.

Slumber was too disappointed to speak, but Rags and Abie argued strongly with Uncle Jasper Tappin. Finally the old man had to threaten to go and bring Abie's father there to get his son if the boy refused to go home.

"Your father will worry hisself sick," he said. Then turning to Slumber, he said, "You can't get people to join your band like that. It ain't right."

Slumber had no answer for Uncle Jasper Tappin, but he felt terrible. The band was broken up. He was tired of Harlem, and he wanted to go home.

XIII

Ripe Persimmons

ABOUT a week later Slumber and his brothers were walking down Seventh Avenue with sandwich boards hanging from their shoulders. The boards reached from their chins to their shoe tops, and on them was written something about where people could have shoes repaired cheaply. A man was going to pay the boys a quarter each for wearing these boards and walking where folks could read the signs.

At first Slumber thought it was going to be a powerfully easy job, just walking up and down streets, but that was before he thought of the sitting down part. Walking is mighty fine when you can stop and take a rest occasionally, but when you're wearing a sandwich board in front and behind there is no chance to rest. And soon Slumber began to dislike his new job.

Furthermore, the boys were still unhappy

about the break-up of their band. Willie was well now, but not well enough to stay out late at night. Aunt Ludy maintained that it was while galavanting around with the band that Willie had caught his cold; and now that he was better, she was not going to let him take any more chances, no matter how many nickels and dimes he missed.

Of course, wearing sandwich boards was better than no job at all. That was why the boys accepted so readily when the man called them into his shop and told them what he had in mind. He promised to pay each of them a quarter if they would stay out all afternoon. When they agreed, he hung the boards over their shoulders, tied some old worn-out shoes to the sides of the boards and sent them out.

After they had walked a short while and turned two or three corners, Slumber paused and waited for his brothers to catch up with him.

"Must be cotton-picking time down home now," he said suddenly.

Rags scratched his head, studying.

"Yes, son, I reckon it is. What put you in mind of it?"

Slumber just blinked his eyes a few times and answered nothing. They had not gone much farther, however, before something else was in his mind. "I expect persimmons be ripe before long — down there."

"Aw, bubber, don't talk about no ripe persimmons," Rags said. "You might make me hungry."

Willie raised his eyes abruptly.

"The old possums will eat every lasting one of the persimmons on that tree down in the low field," he said. "With us way up here there won't be nobody to stop them."

Both Slumber and Rags shook their heads sadly, but they walked another block before either spoke again.

"Big shorty," Slumber said finally, "I'd like to be driving two old mules to the cotton gin right now."

"Hush," Rags said. "You just hush that talk about the cotton gin and ripe persimmons and all like that. Just you hush it up."

"Why?" Willie asked. "I'd rather be riding on a load of cotton, all soft and nice, than walking with this contraption hanging on me."

"If you don't think about something else to talk," Rags said impatiently, "I'm going to stuff a handful of cotton in your mouth."

"Where you going to get the cotton?" Slumber said innocently.

"I tell you hush talking about cotton. I'm going to get mad directly." Rags stamped his foot as he said it, but he did not frighten his brothers.

"Listen," Slumber said. "I feel like going home to Alabama. How about you, Rags."

"Boy, didn't I tell you to hush talking about it. My feet is itching me so bad I can't hardly stand still. And you all just keep talking about persimmons and cotton and the like. If you don't hush it up presently, I'm apt to leave you here."

"Not me, big shorty. You ain't apt to leave me," Slumber said.

"Me neither," Willie assured him.

Then once more each of the boys had his own thoughts and not one had anything to say for a long while. In Slumber's head mighty questions had been turning since the day Aunt Ludy pronounced doom on the band. And now things had come to a turn where he must make a decision. He looked up and saw the leaves falling from the trees along the Avenue and presently a great sadness came to his face. Before he knew it there were tears.

"Do something hurt you, Slumber?" Willie asked kindly.

"No," he said, "nothing don't hurt me."

"What you crying about then?" Rags demanded.

"Nothing," Slumber said. "Just them old trees put me in the mind of something down home."

"What they put you in mind of?" Willie asked, still sympathetic.

"They puts me in mind of some trees down along the pike that runs by home," he said.

Rags waited a moment or two before he said, "They do mind me of home."

"Yes, they do," Willie said.

So for another spell they walked without speaking, but they said no more about Slumber's tears, for Rags and Willie had their own to think about. They made a pitiful picture, these three brothers, walking with their sandwich boards,

'I'M GOING ON BACK DOWN HOME TO ALABAMA'

not talking any more but crying about something that nobody could see.

Finally Slumber stopped and put his foot down emphatically.

"Dog my cats, big shorty, I'm going on back down home to Alabama."

"Me, too," Rags said. "I told you just now that I was apt to leave you all if you didn't stop all that ripe persimmon talk. But no, you just kept right on. I'm ready to leave here, me."

"Uncle Jasper Tappin said he was aiming to take us back with him when he go," Willie suggested.

"I'm tired of waiting for Uncle Jasper Tappin to go," Slumber said impatiently.

"I'm tired too," Rags said. "Let's go up to 409 and tell everybody good-bye."

The other boys murmured a few words.

"We got a heap of nickels and dimes and quarters to help us out this time," Slumber said.

"Yes, we got that dollar bill, too," Willie said.

So up the hill they went, not remembering to take the sandwich boards back to the man who owned them, not looking down at the park or the trees from which the leaves were falling and not minding the stains that were on their faces from crying. They were all smiling now, even Slumber.

On the sidewalk in front of 409 they saw Daisy Bee skating and paused to tell her what was in their minds.

"We leaving you now, Daisy Bee," Slumber said. "So good-bye."

The others nodded that it was true. But Daisy Bee was so surprised and so out of breath there was almost nothing she could say.

"Good-bye," she whispered, not at all happy. "Good-bye, sad-faced boy. Good-bye, you all."

The boys were still excited; they left her on the sidewalk and hurried down to the basement apartment to tell Aunt Ludy and Uncle Jasper Tappin good-bye. But Daisy Bee took off her skates right away and decided she wouldn't play any more that day.

This was not the last she saw of Slumber and his brothers, however. She saw them again a few minutes later, going down the hill to return their sandwich boards to the man who owned them, walking very fast this time, and she watched them till the boards looked no bigger than the pages of a book. Then she saw them turn a corner